A First-Start® Easy Reader

This easy reader contains only 62 different words, repeated often to help the young reader develop word recognition and interest in reading.

a	go	one	table
and	good-night	paint	take
at	help	picture	tell
bath	his	play	the
bed	home	pretty	tick
breakfast	is	Puppy	time
can	it	read	to
clean	just	school	tock
clocks	kiss	set	today
day	let's	share	up
dinner	listen	silly	waiting
do	look	sing	what
dreams	lunch	song	will
eat	Mom	start	you
for	more	story	
get	nap	sweet	

Let's Tell Time

by Melissa Getzoff

illustrated by Julie Durrell

Troll Associates

Tick tock, tick tock. What time is it?

Is it time for Puppy to get up and start his day?

Is it time to eat breakfast?

What will Puppy do at school today?

Is it time to sing a silly song?

Is it time to paint a pretty picture?

Is it time to eat lunch and play?

Is it time to listen to a story?

Is it time for a nap?

Is it time to share?

Is it time to clean up
and go home?

Look! Mom is waiting.

 Is it time to help Mom set the table

Is it time to eat dinner?

Is it time to take a bath?

 Is it time to listen to a story?

Will Mom read just one more?

Is it time for bed…
and a good-night kiss?

Look at the clocks. Can you tell what time it is?

Sweet dreams!